AREN'T WE ALL SPECIAL?

Sharon (Sha') L. Brown

Copyright © 2024 by Sharon (Sha') L. Brown.

All rights reserved. No part of this publication may be reproduced, distributed, or transmitted in any form or by any electronic or mechanical means, including information storage and retrieval systems, without a prior written permission from the publisher, except by reviewers, who may quote brief passages in a review, and certain other noncommercial uses permitted by the copyright law.

Library of Congress Control Number: 2024908604

ISBN: 979-8-89228-146-1   (Paperback)
ISBN: 979-8-89228-147-8   (Hardcover)
ISBN: 979-8-89228-148-5   (eBook)

Printed in the United States of America

I would like to thank God for never leaving or forsaking me throughout my life, and for giving me a heart to love children who are seen as different. I would also like to thank the many children and their families that live daily as Super Heroes with exceptional powers. Not children with disabilities, but children with abilities to find new ways to be successful in life. Remember, you are not different, but unique and it is the rest of the world that is different. I love you, and believe you can you touch higher heights than is ever imagined. Thank you for being my hero.

Sha' L. Brown

"Hayama it's time to wake up for your first day at your new school!" "Thanks Mom!" I'm so excited to go to school today. On yesterday, my mom and dad took me to Open House and I met my new teacher, Miss Stephanie and a new friend, JC.

Mom dropped me off at school and I saw my new friend, JC and our other new friends we met last night. We all walked to class together and put our things away before sitting in our seats.

Introduction!

Our teacher Miss Stephanie starts the class by letting us all introduce ourselves. I told the class about my friend, Jordy. JC told the class about his little brother Jax and his friend, Carlito.

After lunch and recess, Miss Stephanie tells us we are getting a new classmate and that she has a special need. "Special Need?" we asked Miss Stephanie. "Does she have a wheelchair?" "Does she have a hearing aid?" "I thought we were all special?" We had so many questions for Miss Stephanie.

"Yes, you are all special", said Miss Stephanie. "Special needs mean that our new friend needs extra help in some areas that may be easier for others. There are many different types of special needs. Some of them you can see with your eyes like a wheelchair, and some you cannot see with your eyes. Either way, being different should not mean being treated differently. We all need good friends.

There is a knock at the door. The Principal, Mr. Marvin introduces our new classmate, Sara and her parents. Sara doesn't look like she needs extra help. She looks just like the rest of us. Then I remembered Miss Stephanie said some differences you can't see with your eyes.

Miss Stephanie seats Sara next to me. She asks if I could be her friend and help her get settled. Sara and I had fun working together. It's time for reading, and Sara has difficulty with many of the words.

Miss Stephanie came over and explained that Sara has trouble processing words. Miss Stephanie said we can all do our part by helping Sara in class. This is what makes us all special because we work together and help each other!

Later at home, I told my mom and dad all about our new friend, Sara. I told them she had a hard time reading, but I am going to be a good friend and help her every day. I asked if Sara could come over sometimes and play. My mom is so proud of me for being a great friend. She said I am really a special friend. Wow! So, we really are all special!

About The Author

Sharon (Sha) L. Brown was born in a small town in South Carolina called Barnwell. She is the youngest of eight children; five girls and three boys born to the late Edgar & Eunice Brown. She obtained her Undergraduate degree from the University of South Carolina in Interdisciplinary studies with a minor in Sociology. She obtained her Master's degree in Special Education from the University of Arizona, and plans to continue using her talent, education, and skills to help others. She is currently pursuing a Doctoral degree in Theology from Ecumenical University, and serving as a Special Education Teacher. She is very involved in building up her community and has volunteered with nonprofit organizations to include; The National Alliance on Mental Illness (NAMI), Red Cross, and the Save the Children Action Network (SCAN). She has also served as a Guardian Ad Litem, Red Cross Health & Safety Instructor, and Victim Advocate. She has a heart for service and she illustrates this by advocating and providing meals and clothing to the homeless and displaced several times a year.

Sha' has written, produced, and directed eight original plays. She has published two children's books, Goodbye Friend, and What Will Happen to Jojo. She has served as Production Manager, and Executive Manager for JBStar Productions for fifteen years on various stage and screen productions. She recently served as First AD with JBStar Production on the project, "Ain't No Power Like Prayer". Sha' has also served as Production Manager/ Assistant Producer with Sage Rage Productions for the movie, "Contrary Lee Speaking".

Sha' is mom to four wonderful military brats and Abuela (grandmother) to five amazing grandchildren of which four are military brats. She has worked for the Department of Defense for fifteen years in the Child and Youth Services Division. Everyone who knows her knows that she has a calling for working with children, and children respond to her in a very positive manner. She has experienced the heartache and pain military children go through from a service viewpoint, as well as, from a parent's view point. She has seen the effects Deployments, Permanent Change of Station (PCS), and Temporary Duty assignments have on a family, especially on the child (ren). She has always been particularly concerned for children and youth with special needs or exceptionalities who are affected even more due to their difficulty in expressing the feelings they are experiencing. The Pee Wee Warriors series was birthed through Sha's heart from God knowing the challenges children with and without exceptionalities go through daily. Sha' continues to advocate for children and youth with and without exceptionalities, and will never give up on being a positive part of the lives of children and youth in any capacity she can.

Milton Keynes UK
Ingram Content Group UK Ltd.
UKHW052109050824
446596UK00002B/6